AF437532

Mary Black

Journey to the Sun

Joy was standing at the window of her room awaiting eagerly Didi, the good fairy. After their journey in Fairyland, Didi had promised to Joy a travel to the Kingdom of Sun.

So, as soon as Joy saw Didi, her face shined with happiness.

"Hi, Joy!" The little fairy said.

"I was waiting for you." Joy responded.

"Sorry I'm late, but I had to ask for King Sun to give us permission to visit his Kingdom."

"Did he give it?" asked Joy, full of anxiety.

"Look!" Didi exclaimed, pointing out to Joy a piece of an ancient papyrus written in golden letters:

-Are you ready to go? Asked Didi.

-Yes, yes! Responded Joy.

The good fairy threw fairy dust to Joy, then
took her hand and they began to fly high into
the sky. Our little
friend felt as if she
had her own wings.
They flew for some
time until they landed
on a cloud.

-This is Horace said
Didi.
-Hello! Exclaimed the
beautiful cloud with
his velvety voice.
-Horace will carry us to the Kingdom of Sun,
said Didi. But we have to wait for Mr. Wind.

It's too hot up there and someone has to cool us.

Soon they heard a strange sound and a sweet breeze freshened them.

Mr. Wind welcomed our friends with a blast.

Didi and Joy sat comfortably  in Horace, and the lovely cloud began to rise gently and full of grace and suppleness into the sky.

-*How soft he is!* Joy thought. It was the most beautiful cloud she had ever seen.

Their journey was quiet and comfortable.

They traveled between the other clouds, who greeted them with enthusiasm.

Some were white, othere were grayer, ready

tbring the rain.

Some were small and

others large.

Everyone was beautiful,

no matter what shape,

size or color they were.

Suddenly, they heard a voice behind them

saying:

-Horace, my child where are you going?

-Hello Mother,

little Horace said

enthusiastically.

-Where are you

going? asked

again mom Cloud full of concern.

-I must carry Didi and her friend Joy to the Kingdom of Sun.

- Take care, my son! Don't get lost on your way! Mom Cloud said.

-Don't worry mom, I know how to get back. I've put the sign on Blow and

Clod. They always stay in the same position. It is still Summer and they may not be moved. If they shake even a little they will immediately become rain and Captain Cloud will

be angry.He intends to use them for first rain and they would not lose this opportunity for anything, mom Cloud said laughing.

-Mom, When will I become first rain? Horace asked.

-When you grow up and you become obedient, Captain Cloud might entrust to you such a task.

-Oh, how much I'd like to become first rain! the little Horace exclaimed.

-Why do you want to be first rain? Joy asked him in wonder.

-Because it is a gentle rain that everyone likes: the thirsty earth, the trees, the flowers, the birds and the animals.

Humans also like it! All creatures thirsty and tired of the Summer's heat, ask for the first rain as a divine blessing, answered Horace.

-Doesn't it depress you to become rain and cease to be a cloud? Our little friend asked Horace.

-Not at all! he replied.

While they were travelling through the sky, dozens of stars came close to them. They did pirouettes leaving a glowing tail behind them.

 Joy was amazed by the sight. One of the stars approached her and said:

-My name is Nelly. Do you want me to become
your star?
-I'd love that!
replied our little
friend.
-From now on, I'll be
your bright star and
I'll follow you

everywhere, Nelly said.
-How will I stand out among so many others?
Joy asked the little star.
 -For you I will be the brightest, Nelly said.
Then she made a pirouette and went back to
the other stars.

After quite a bit of time spent travelling,

Horace rose into the sky, until it began to get

very hot.

Mr. Wind started blowing loudly to cool them

down.

-We arrived, Didi said, after a while.

Horace landed at the
entrance to the
Kingdom of Sun.
When they went
down, our little
friend saw a
golden palace.

She went ahead following Didi until they
arrived in front of the entrance of the palace.
The little fairy knocked on the door and when
it opened, they saw a beautiful sunbeam
before them.

-Welcome, she told them. I am one of the Sun's
daughters and my name is
Merope. Come in! My
father is expecting
you, Merope said and
she led them to a huge
room bathed in light. In

the center, there was an ornate golden throne.
A thousand year old man sat regally on the
throne.

He wore a glittering mantle embroidered with
precious stones.

He had long, auburn, wavy golden hair and
elegnat beard.

His head was crowned with a radial diadem.

He had a bright and
hospitable personality
and he reminded Joy
of her grandfather.
A huge globe was
beside him. Right
and left of him dozens
of Sunbeams were sitting.
-Welcome to my Kingdom, he, said with
booming voice. Get closer!
 Joy and Didi approached King Sun and knelt
before him respectfully.

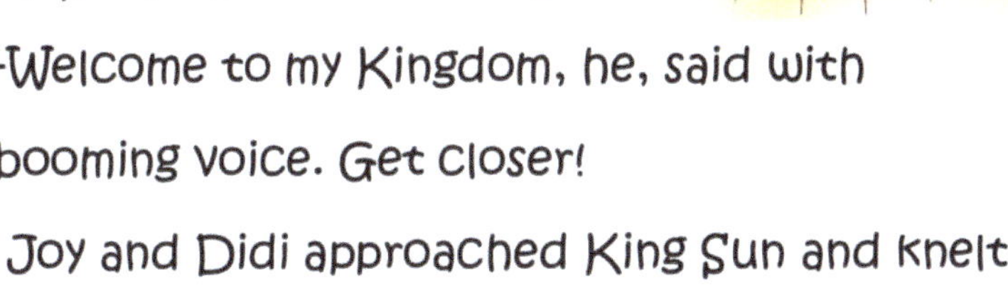

Our little friend said:

-King Sun! Nice to meet you. Thank you for allowing me to visit your Kingdom.

-My Pleasure! Sun replied. Although I am angry with you people.

-Why; Joy asked him.

-Why, centuries now, I send my sons and my daughters, the

Sunbeams, to illuminate you, and vitalize you and help flourish your planet, but you, you ungrateful Earth People, you pollute and destroy it.

I'm so angry with you that sometimes it goes through my mind to descend to Earth and burn you. When you go back to earth, give this message to the people:

Be more attentive and sensitive to the goods

that nature generously gives you. Do not

destroy this beautiful planet in the name of

'development', as you say!

Someday I will get so angry that I'll

stop sending my light and warmth to earth!

 While his voice was very angry and jets of small

flames spat with every word, Joy realized that

King Sun was right and he was angry for the

sake of humanity.

-Come closer the king said, so I can introduce

you to my sons and daughters.

This is Phoebe, said King Sun showing a

graceful Sunbeam, who was sitting at his feet.

On my Right, is Lampiris. On the left, is

Essential and Glamour. Behind

me are my sons

Phaeton, the shiner

Aeetes and Kerkafos.

These are my daughters

Dioxippi, and Circe and this is my little

sweetheart Heliodorus, who

will accompany you to see

my chariot with immortal

winged horses.

Hurry! You have to leave before dawn.

Didi and Joy thanked King Sun and followed Heliodorus. Around the palace there were hundreds of small houses.

-What are these? Joy asked.

-Our houses, replied Heliodorus the Sunbeam.

-Why are some of them brighter and others less so? Joy asked.

-In brightest houses, daytime Sunbeams are living which are the hottest and brightest, and in the less bright houses, are midday Sunbeams, which are less bright.

Heliodorus led them to the back side of the palace.

There were stables, where the favorite
horses of King Sun were staying. Heliodorus
opened a big door and Joy saw a golden
glittering chariot.

The wheels of the
chariot were
made of golden
flames.
Four horses were
tied onto the
chariot.
They were breathing light and flames from
their nostrils.
They had white wings and golden reins.
 -They are wonderful! exclaimed our little
friend with admiration.

Heliodorus approached the horses, stroked them tenderly and said:

-These are Shining, Flash, Red and Fiery.

-What do they eat? Joy asked.

-A magical herb that grows in the valley beyond, Heliodorus replied.

-Joy, we must go, said Didi. Soon, it will be dawn.

Heliodorus bided farewell to Didi and Joy. Horace the cloud and Mr. Wind were waiting for them at the entrance.

Before the King Sun shed its first rays on earth, Joy was back in her room. As she was staring at the sunrise, she wondered if her journey to the Kingdom of King Sun was true or just one of her beautiful dreams she saw every night. The voice of her mother took her from her thoughts. She dressed and went down for breakfast.

 She had to spread King Sun's message for humanity.

Do not destroy the planet Earth

in the name of development!

-Hello my friends!
I am Nino the plant. I live in the forest. Please, save our forests. Please save me!

OUR PLANET IS SO AMAZINING

SAVE IT
PROTECT IT

ONe
HOME